The Girl Who
Loved the Wind

For David Stemple and Steve Yolen,
brothers of the wind

The Girl
Who Loved
the Wind

by
Jane Yolen
pictures by
Ed Young

THOMAS Y. CROWELL COMPANY
New York   Established 1834

Published simultaneously in Canada by
Fitzhenry & Whiteside, Limited, Toronto.
Calligraphy by Ray Barber

Printed in Belgium

L.C. Card 71-171012
ISBN 0-690-33100-2

0-690-33101-0 (LB)

Once many years ago in a country far to the east there lived a wealthy merchant. He was a widower and had an only daughter named Danina. She was dainty and beautiful, and he loved her more than he loved all of his treasures.

Because Danina was his only child, the merchant wanted to keep her from anything that might hurt or harm her in any way, and so he decided to shut her away from the world.

When Danina was still an infant, her father brought her to a great house which he had built on the shore of the sea. On three sides of the house rose three huge walls. And on the fourth side was the sea itself.

In this lovely, lonely place Danina grew up knowing every-

thing that was in her father's heart but nothing of the world.

In her garden grew every kind of fair fruit and flower, for so her father willed it. And on her table was every kind of fresh fish and fowl, for so her father ordered. In her room were the finest furnishings. Gaily colored books and happy music, light dancing and bright paintings, filled her days. And the servants were instructed always to smile, never to say no, and to be cheerful all through the year. So her father wished it and so it was done. And for many years, nothing sad touched Danina in any way.

Yet one spring day, as Danina stood by her window gazing at the sea, a breeze blew salt across the waves. It whipped her hair about her face. It blew in the corners of her room. And as it moved, it whistled a haunting little tune.

Danina had never heard such a thing before. It was sad, but it was beautiful. It intrigued her. It beguiled her. It caused her to sigh and clasp her hands.

"Who are you?" asked Danina.

And the wind answered:

Who am I?
I call myself the wind.
I slap at ships and sparrows.
I sough through broken windows.
I shepherd snow and sandstorms.
I am not always kind.

"How peculiar," said Danina. "Here you merely rustle the trees and play with the leaves and calm the birds in their nests."

"*I am not always kind,*" said the wind again.

"Everyone here is always kind. Everyone here is always happy."

"*Nothing is always,*" said the wind.

"My life is always," said Danina. "Always happy."

"*But life is not always happy,*" said the wind.

"Mine is," said Danina.

"*How sad,*" whispered the wind from a corner.

"What do you mean?" asked Danina. But the wind only whirled through the window carrying one of her silken scarves, and before she could speak again, he had blown out to sea.

Days went by, happy days. Yet sometimes in her room, Danina would try to sing the wind's song. She could not quite remember the words or recall the tune, but its strangeness haunted her.

Finally, one morning, she asked

her father: "Why isn't life always happy?"

"Life *is* always happy," replied her father.

"That's what I told him," said Danina.

"Told who?" asked her father. He was suddenly frightened,

frightened that someone would take his daughter away.

"The wind," said Danina.

"The wind does not talk," said her father.

"He called himself the wind," she replied.

But her father did not understand. And so when a passing fisherman found Danina's scarf far

out at sea and returned it to the
merchant's house, he was rewarded

with a beating, for the merchant
suspected that the fisherman was
the one who called himself the
wind.

Then one summer day, weeks later, when the sun was reflected in the petals of the flowers, Danina strolled in her garden. Suddenly the wind leaped over the high wall and pushed and pulled at the tops of the trees. He sang his strange song, and Danina clasped her hands and sighed.

"Who are you?" she whispered.

"*Who am I?*" said the wind, and he sang:

Who am I?
I call myself the wind.
I've worked the sails of windmills.
I've whirled the sand in deserts.
I've wrecked ten thousand galleons.
I am not always kind.

"I knew it was you," said Danina. "But no one believed me."

And the wind danced around the garden and made the flowers bow.

He caressed the birds in the trees and played gently with the feathers on their wings.

"You say you are not always kind," said Danina. "You say you have done many unkind things. But all I see is that you are gentle and good."

"*But not always,*" reminded the wind. "*Nothing is always.*"

"Is it sad then beyond the wall?"

"*Sometimes sad and sometimes happy,*" said the wind.

"But different each day?" said Danina.

"*Very different.*"

"How strange," Danina said. "Here things are always the same. Always beautiful. Happy. Good."

"*How sad,*" said the wind. "*How dull.*" And he leaped over the wall and blew out into the world.

"Come back," shouted Danina, rushing to the wall. But her voice was lost against the stones.

Just then her father came into the garden. He saw his daughter standing by the wall and crying to the top. He ran over to her. "Who are you calling? Who has been here?" he demanded.

"The wind," said Danina, her eyes bright with memory. "He sang me his song."

"The wind does not sing," said her father. "Only men and birds sing."

"This was no bird," said his daughter.

"Then," thought her father, "it must have been a man." And he resolved to keep Danina from the garden.

Locked out of her garden, Danina began to wander up and down the long corridors of the house, and what once had seemed like a palace to her began to feel like a prison. Everything seemed false. The happy smiles of the servants she saw as smiles of pity for her ignorance. The gay dancing seemed to hide broken hearts. The bright paintings hid sad thoughts. And soon Danina found herself thinking of the wind at every moment, humming his song to the walls. His song about the world—sometimes happy, sometimes sad, but always full of change and challenge.

Her father, who was not cruel but merely foolish, could not keep her locked up completely. Once a day, for an hour, he allowed Danina to walk along the beach. But three maidservants walked before her. Three manservants walked behind. And the merchant himself watched from a covered chair.

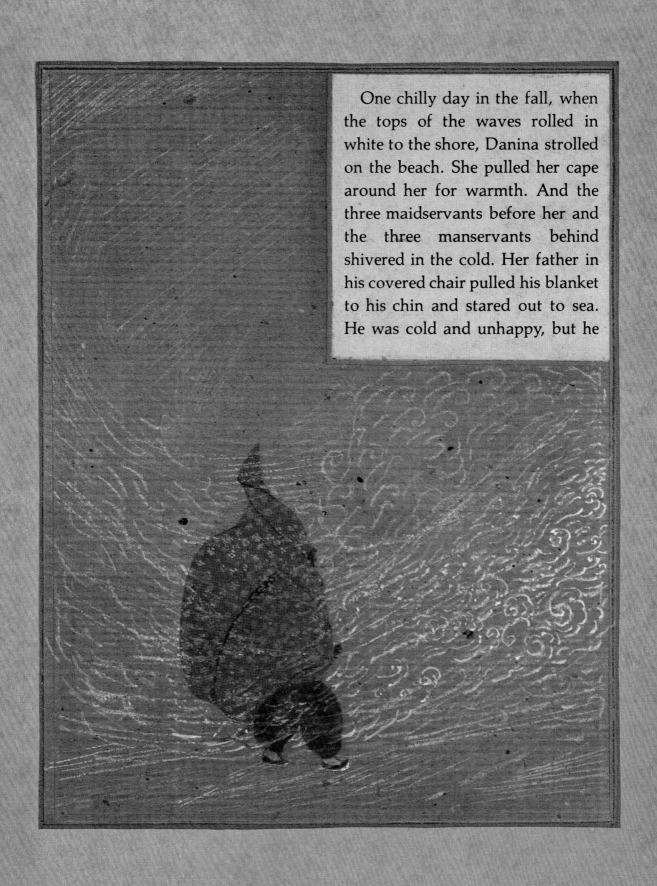

One chilly day in the fall, when the tops of the waves rolled in white to the shore, Danina strolled on the beach. She pulled her cape around her for warmth. And the three maidservants before her and the three manservants behind shivered in the cold. Her father in his covered chair pulled his blanket to his chin and stared out to sea. He was cold and unhappy, but he

was more afraid to leave Danina alone.

Suddenly the wind blew across the caps of the waves, tossing foam into the air.

Danina turned to welcome him, stretching out her arms. The cape billowed behind her like the wings of a giant bird.

"Who are you?" thundered Danina's father, jumping out of his chair.

The wind spun around Danina and sang:

Who am I?
I call myself the wind.
I am not always happy.
I am not always kind.

"Nonsense," roared Danina's father. "Everyone here is always happy and kind. I shall arrest you for trespassing." And he shouted, "GUARDS!"

But before the guards could come, Danina had spread her cape

on the water. Then she stepped onto it, raised one corner, and waved good-bye to her father. The blowing wind filled the cape's corner like the sail of a ship.

And before Danina's father had time to call out, before he had time for one word of repentance, she was gone. And the last thing he saw was the billowing cape as Danina and the wind sailed far to the west into the ever-changing world.

About the author

Jane Yolen, born in New York, was graduated from Smith College. She now lives with her husband and their three small children in a lovely old house in Hatfield, Massachusetts. She worked for a time as an editor of children's books with a large New York publisher before deciding to devote herself to writing. She is also an accomplished folk singer, often accompanying herself on the guitar, autoharp, and fairy bells.

Among Jane Yolen's many distinguished books for young people are *The Bird of Time*, illustrated by Mercer Mayer, and the award-winning *Emperor and the Kite*, illustrated by Ed Young.

About the illustrator

Ed Young was born in China and spent his childhood in Shanghai. When he came to the United States, he studied at the University of Illinois and at the Art Center School in Los Angeles. He now lives in New York City. In addition to his art, he has a deep interest in Tai Chi Chuan.

His pictures for *The Girl Who Loved the Wind* are reminiscent of Persian miniatures in their richly patterned design, but his technique—a mixture of watercolor and collage— is completely modern and was developed especially for this book.